Adventures with

BANANAS IN PAJAMAS ™

Ratmobile · Something Fishy · Bedtime
written by Richard Tulloch

Banana Hiccups · Painted Bananas · House Sitter
written by Simon Hopkinson

Illustrated by Nick Watson

Random House New York

Library of Congress Catalog Card Number: 96-70622
ISBN 0-679-88600-1

http://www.randomhouse.com/

Printed in the United States of America
10 9 8 7 6 5 4 3 2 1

BANANAS IN PAJAMAS is a trademark of the
Australian Broadcasting Corporation.

CONTENTS

RATMOBILE

One morning, Rat in a Hat's special Ratmobile broke down!

RAT·1

Chugga-chugga-CLUNK! went the Ratmobile.
"Oh, cheese and whiskers!" said Rat in a Hat.

Just then, Amy arrived on her scooter.
"Hello, Rat," said Amy. "I'm riding
my scooter to the beach. But it's
harder work than driving a car."

7

"Amy, this could be your lucky day," said Rat in a Hat.
"I'll swap you the Ratmobile for your scooter. Then you can drive to the beach in style."

"Are you sure?" asked Amy.

"Trust me, I'm a rat," said Rat in a Hat.

So Rat in a Hat rode off on Amy's scooter.

Amy climbed into the Ratmobile. When she tried to start the car…

Chugga-chugga-CLUNK! went the Ratmobile.

Just then, the Bananas in Pajamas arrived.
Chugga-chugga-CLUNK! went the Ratmobile.
"Are you thinking what I'm thinking, B1?" asked B2.
"I think I am, B2," said B1. "It's Fixing Time!"

B1 lifted the hood of the Ratmobile.
B2 adjusted the motor with a screwdriver.
B1 tapped the motor with a hammer.
Chugga-chugga-BANG! went the Ratmobile.

Lulu was walking to the beach. She saw Amy and the Bananas trying to start the Ratmobile.
"Perhaps it's out of gas," said Lulu.
"What a good idea!" said B1 and B2.

The Bananas poured gas into the Ratmobile. Chugga-chugga-VROOM-VROOM! went the Ratmobile. And they all drove to the beach.

Rat in a Hat was already at the beach.
But he was tired. He wasn't used to all that exercise.
Amy's scooter <u>was</u> hard work!

When Rat in a Hat heard that the Ratmobile had only run out of gas, he wanted it back again. "If you give it back," he said to Amy, "I'll give you the scooter <u>and</u> a new beach tube, too."

Amy didn't mind. She wanted her scooter to play with on the beach. Lulu wanted the new tube to play with in the water. They gave Rat in a Hat the keys to the Ratmobile and scooted down to the beach.

Rat in a Hat was happy to have his car back. He rubbed his hands together and hummed to himself as he turned the key.

Chugga-chugga-CLUNK! went the Ratmobile.
"Oh, cheese and whiskers!" said Rat in a Hat. "It's broken down again."
And he had to push the Ratmobile all the way home!

BANANA HICCUPS

One morning, the Bananas in Pajamas were coming down the stairs. Suddenly, B1 went <u>hic-CUP</u>!

"Oh, dear!" he said. "I think I've got a case of the hiccups!"

"Oh, dear!" said B2. "What do you do to get rid of the hiccups?"

<u>Hic-CUP</u>! went B1 again. "I don't know," he said.

So the Bananas went next door to ask the Teddies if they knew how to get rid of the hiccups.

"Take a deep breath and jump up and down as hard as you can," said Amy.

So B1 took a deep breath and jumped up and down as hard as he could.

"There you go," said Amy when B1 stopped jumping. "It works every time!"

<u>Hic-CUP</u>! went B1.

"Hmm," said Amy. "Perhaps it only works for Teddies! I'll go find Morgan. He might know how to get rid of the hiccups."

Just then, Lulu walked in. The Bananas asked Lulu if she knew how to get rid of the hiccups.

"Stand on your head and drink a glass of water very, very slowly," said Lulu with great confidence.

So B1 stood on his head and drank a glass of water upside down very, very slowly.

"Well done, B1," said B2. "You didn't spill a drop."
Lulu and B2 helped B1 to his feet.

<u>Hic-CUP</u>! went B1.
"I can't understand it," said Lulu. "That always works for me!"

Just then, Amy ran through the back door.

"Don't worry, B1. Morgan and I will get rid of your hiccups. All you have to do is open the front door!"

"How will that get rid of my hiccups?" asked B1.

"You'll see," said Amy with a smile.

So B1 opened the door—and in leaped Morgan wearing a scary mask!

"BOO!" yelled Morgan.

"Oh!" cried the Bananas as they jumped back in fright.

"It's all right, Bananas," said Morgan as he pulled off the mask. "It's only me!"

"You scared us!" said B1.

"That was the idea—to frighten away your hiccups!" said Morgan.

"It worked!" shouted B1 with glee. "My hiccups are gone!"
"Well done, Morgan!" said Amy.
B1 turned to B2. "What about that, B2? My hiccups have gone!"
Hic-CUP! went B2. "Now I have the hiccups!"

PAINTED BANANAS

One day, Amy was drawing Lulu's picture. It was very hard to draw. Lulu just wouldn't stand still. When Morgan walked in, he burst out laughing. "That picture looks like a mop!"

"I don't look anything like that!" Lulu said when she saw the picture.
"I bet you can't draw a better picture," said Amy.

So the Teddies decided to have a drawing contest.
Later that morning, the Bananas in Pajamas were down on the beach.
Morgan ran up to them. He had something very important to ask the Bananas.
"May I draw your picture?" Morgan asked.
"We'd be delighted!" the Bananas said to Morgan.

Morgan asked B1 to sit on a rock. He asked B2 to stand behind the rock with his hand on B1's shoulder.
Then Morgan started his drawing.

That afternoon, the Bananas in Pajamas were at home.
Amy knocked on the door.
"I want to draw your picture," said Amy.

So Amy asked B1 to sit on the couch. She asked B2 to stand
behind the couch with his hand on B1's shoulder.
Then Amy started her drawing.

The next morning, the Bananas in Pajamas were in the park when Lulu came up to them and asked if she could draw their picture.

Lulu asked B1 to sit on the bench and B2 to stand behind the bench with his hand on B1's shoulder.
And then she started her drawing.

That afternoon, the Teddies invited the Bananas in Pajamas to be the judges for their drawing contest.

"We've each drawn a picture," explained Amy.

"And we'd like you to decide which one is the best," added Lulu.

At a signal from Morgan, the three Teddies uncovered their drawings.
The Bananas looked at all the pictures and burst out laughing.

The pictures were all exactly the same!
Lulu, Morgan, and Amy looked at each other and laughed, too.
"Everyone is a winner!" declared B1 and B2.
And the Teddies never argued again over who could draw the
best picture.

SOMETHING FISHY

Lulu had a brand-new fishing rod. "Don't bother going shopping today," she said to Morgan and Amy. "I'll catch some fish for our dinner tonight."

"But you don't know how to catch fish, Lulu," said Amy.
"Nonsense," said Lulu. "Fishing is easy. Anyone can do it!"
So off she went to the beach with her fishing rod over her shoulder.

But catching fish wasn't so easy after all. At the end of the day, Lulu's basket was empty.

"Oh, dear," she sighed. "I can't go home without any fish. What will we eat for our dinner?"

Meanwhile, the Bananas had caught a whole basket of fish at their secret fishing spot. When they saw how sad Lulu was, they showed her how to cast her line and reel it in.

"All right," said Lulu. "I'll give it a try!"

But as Lulu got ready to fish, the Bananas had an idea.

"Are you thinking what I'm thinking, B1?" whispered B2.

"I think I am, B2," B1 whispered back.

"It's Trick Time!"

The Bananas took their basket of fish behind a sand dune. When Lulu cast her line, the Bananas took a fish out of their basket and quickly hooked it onto Lulu's line.

Lulu reeled her line in.

"A fish!" cried Lulu. "I've really caught a fish!"

But one fish wasn't enough for the Teddies' dinner.

So Lulu cast her line again.

And the Bananas hooked another fish onto Lulu's line.

She reeled it in again.

"Another fish!" cried Lulu.

Just then, Morgan came down to the beach.
"I told you fishing was easy!" said Lulu. She showed Morgan how to cast the line.
Behind the sand dune, the tricky Bananas in Pajamas were having trouble.
They couldn't get the fish to stay on Lulu's fishing line. Lulu pulled and pulled.

"It feels like a shark!"
puffed Lulu.
"It looks like…two
Bananas in Pajamas!" said
Morgan.

"You tricksters!" said Lulu.
"I thought I was catching
those fish all by myself."
So the Bananas in
Pajamas gave Lulu some
special worms and told her
about their secret fishing
spot.

That night, Lulu and Morgan came home singing a fish-catching song.

"Big fish and fat fish, long fish and flat fish. Fish by the basketload to eat for our dinner…"

Amy ran out to meet them. "What did you catch?"

Lulu opened the basket. Inside were three fish, just enough for the Teddies' dinner.

"And we really caught them all by ourselves!" said Lulu.

HOUSE SITTER

The Bananas in Pajamas were going on vacation. As they were waiting for the bus on Cuddles Avenue, Rat in a Hat came out of his shop.

"Going on vacation, Bananas? Have you got your tickets?" asked Rat.

"Right here," said the Bananas.

"And your toothbrush and toothpaste?" asked Rat.

"Right here," said the Bananas.

"And someone to look after your house while you're away?" asked Rat.

"No," said B1 and B2.

With a smile, Rat produced a big badge from his pocket. The words on the badge read, <u>Rat in a Hat, Official House Sitter. Reasonable Rates</u>.

"I'll take care of your house. Trust me, I'm a rat," grinned Rat in a Hat.

"Oh, thank you!" said B1 and B2.

Rat in a Hat moved into the Bananas' house. He dumped his clothes in a big heap on the floor. Then he went to the kitchen to find something to eat.

"There must be something tasty here somewhere," he muttered as he rummaged through the shelves.

"Munchy honey cakes! Oooh, yum!" Rat licked his lips, opened the jar, and stuffed a munchy honey cake into his mouth.

One week later, Lulu went to the Bananas' house.

When Rat in a Hat opened the front door, Lulu was very surprised.

Everything was a terrible mess. There were pizza boxes, hamburger wrappings, and empty soda cans lying all over the floor!

"Look at this place!" she said. "What a terrible mess!"

Lulu turned to Rat in a Hat.

"You <u>are</u> going to clean everything up before the Bananas get back, aren't you, Rat?"

"Me? Well, I'm very busy…" stuttered Rat.

"Busy doing what? Sleeping, eating, and making a very big mess?" asked Lulu.

"Oh, cheese and whiskers!" muttered Rat.

So, under Lulu's watchful eye, Rat in a Hat cleaned up the Bananas' house. First he picked up the garbage. Then he dusted the furniture and scrubbed the floors.

At last it was all done. Rat in a Hat was exhausted. He fell onto the couch just as the Bananas walked in the front door.

The Bananas looked around their house.
"My goodness! Look how clean everything is, B2!"
"And look how neat and tidy everything is, B1!"
"It's a good thing we hired an official house sitter!" said B1 and B2.
"Yes," agreed Lulu, trying not to laugh.

The Bananas went to thank Rat in a Hat for taking such good care of their house. But he was fast asleep!

BED TIME

The Bananas in Pajamas were very excited. Tomorrow they were going on a camping trip with the Teddies.

They'd spent all day packing their backpacks. At last they were finished.
"I'm tired, B1," said B2.
"I'm very, <u>very</u> tired, B2," said B1. "Maybe we should go to bed."
"Good idea, B1," said B2.
So they went upstairs to bed.

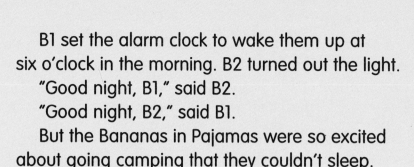

B1 set the alarm clock to wake them up at
six o'clock in the morning. B2 turned out the light.
"Good night, B1," said B2.
"Good night, B2," said B1.
But the Bananas in Pajamas were so excited
about going camping that they couldn't sleep.
They tossed and turned, and they turned and
tossed.

Then they sat up. "Maybe we should read for a little while, B1," said B2.
"Good idea, B2," said B1.
B2 switched on the light, and they read their books all the way through.
Then they lay down to sleep again.

But the Bananas tossed and turned, and they turned and tossed. Then they sat up.
"Are you thinking what I'm thinking, B1?" asked B2.
"I think I am, B2," said B1.
"It's Glass of Milk Time!"

41

The Bananas went down to the kitchen for some milk. They hoped that drinking milk would make them sleepy.

Then they climbed into bed, switched off the light, and settled down to sleep.

"Good night, B1," said B2.

"Good night, B2," said B1.

But they tossed and turned and turned and tossed. Then they sat up.

"We'll have to count ourselves to sleep, B1!" said B2.

"Good idea, B2," said B1.

But the Bananas weren't very good at counting.

"Seven, nine, eighteen, forty, a hundred, six, twenty-one…" counted B2, who was getting very, very sleepy.

Just then…

Bing-bong! went the doorbell. The Bananas sat up in their beds.
"Yoo-hoo! Anyone home?" called the Teddies as they knocked on the Bananas' back door.

The Teddies had been so excited about going camping that they couldn't sleep, either. "Look what we've brought you," said Morgan.
"Munchy honey cakes!" said B1.
"A whole box of them!" said B2.
"Thank you, Teddies!" said B1 and B2.

The Bananas and the Teddies stayed up late, eating munchy honey cakes.

When they'd finished the last munchy honey cake, the Bananas said good night to the Teddies.

But they were so very tired that they only got halfway up the stairs before…they…fell…asleep!